Little Fern's First Winter

Jane Simmons

ORCHARD BOOKS

D0453001

For James, Maria and Gabriel

ORCHARD BOOKS
96 Leonard Street, London EC2A 4XD
Orchard Books Australia
Unit 31/56 O'Riordan Street, Alexandria NSW 2015
1 86039 988 6 (hardback)
1 84121 612 7 (paperback)
First published in Great Britain in 2000
First paperback publication in 2001
Copyright © Jane Simmons 2000
The right of Jane Simmons to be identified as the author and illustrator of this work has been
asserted by her in accordance with the Copyright, Designs and Patents Act, 1988.
A CIP catalogue record for this book is available from the British Library.
1 2 3 4 5 6 7 8 9 10 (hardback)
2 3 4 5 6 7 8 9 10 (paperback)
Printed in Singapore

"The snow is coming!" said Ma Rabbit.

"What's snow?" said Fern.

"Lovely fluffy stuff when it settles, but very very cold," said Ma. "Go and play with Bracken while I change the hay."

Fern and Bracken hopped and
flipped and giggled together.
"Let's play hide and seek,"
said Fern. "I'll hide first."
"And I'll count," said
Bracken. "1, 2, 3, 4 . . ."

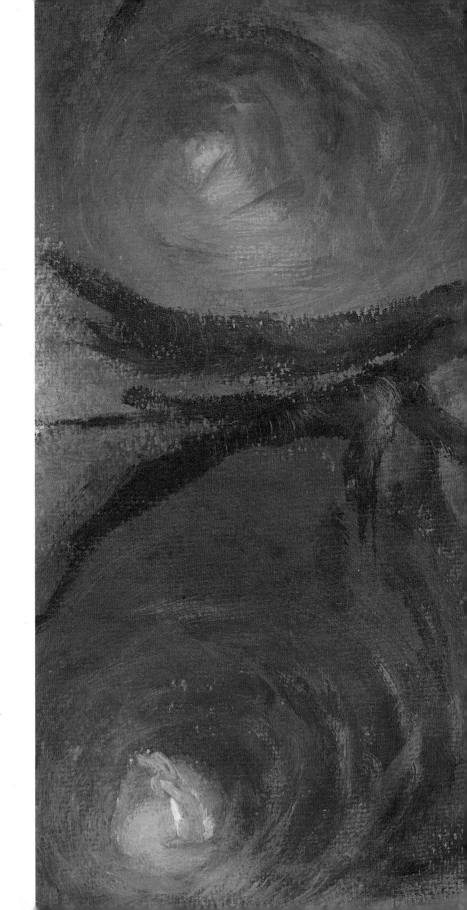

Fern looked for somewhere to hide.
All the birds were swooping and chattering.
  "The snow is coming! We must fly away!"
they squawked.

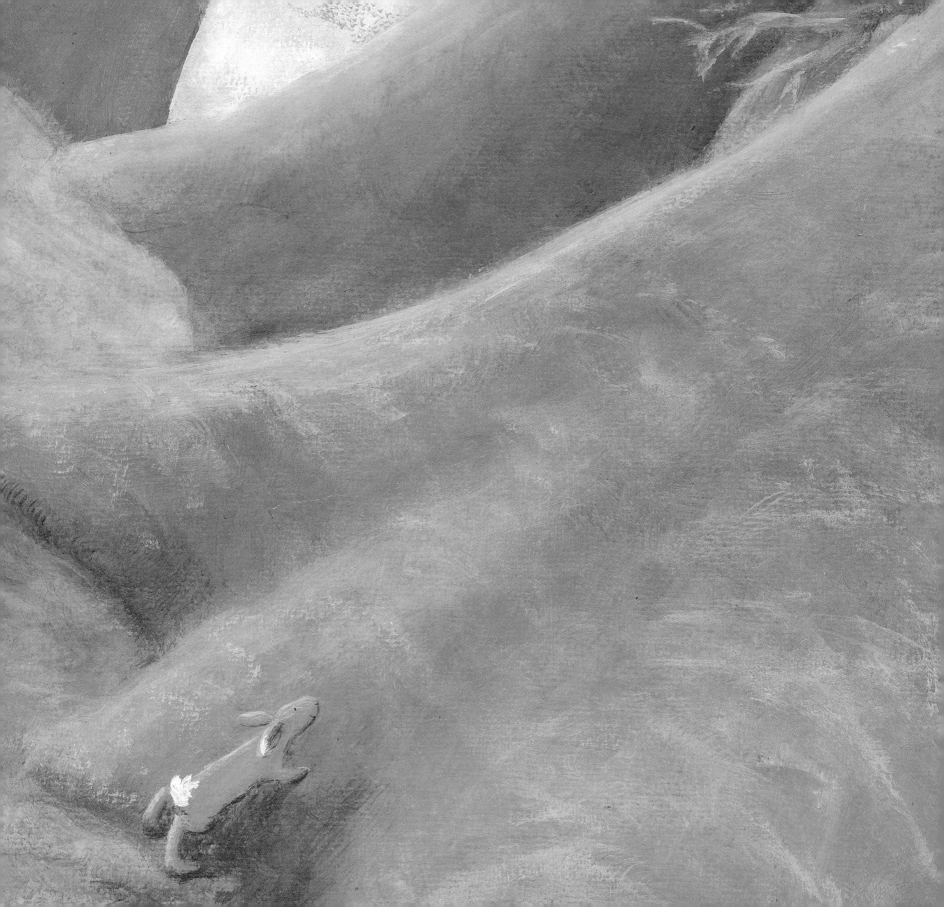

"Can I hide in your store?" asked Fern.

"No. The snow is coming! We need our store for our nuts," said squirrel.

So Fern hopped on.

"Can I hide in your nest?" Fern asked the mice.
"The snow is coming! We need to sleep in our
nest until it's warmer," they said.

"Can I hide with
you?" she asked
the beetles, but
they just crept away.

Fern couldn't find
anywhere to hide.

"Found you!" shouted Bracken. And
they hopped and flipped and giggled
together.

   "Now it's your turn to hide," said Fern,
and she started to count.

"1, 2, 3, 4, 5, 6, 7, 8 . . ."

"...9, 10! I'm coming!"
she shouted.
Everything was quiet in the wood.

There were no birds in the sky . . .   no squirrels in the tree . . .

no mice in the grass . . .

no beetles under the leaves . . .

and no Bracken
anywhere!

Fern went down the burrow under the ground.

"Ma, have you seen Bracken?" asked Fern.

"No, dear," said Ma Rabbit. "I've been changing the hay."

So Fern went up the burrow and outside again.

"Bracken, where are you?" said Fern. A chill wind whistled through the silent wood. Fern shivered.

"Bracken!" she called. Something cold and soft melted on her nose.

"Bracken!"

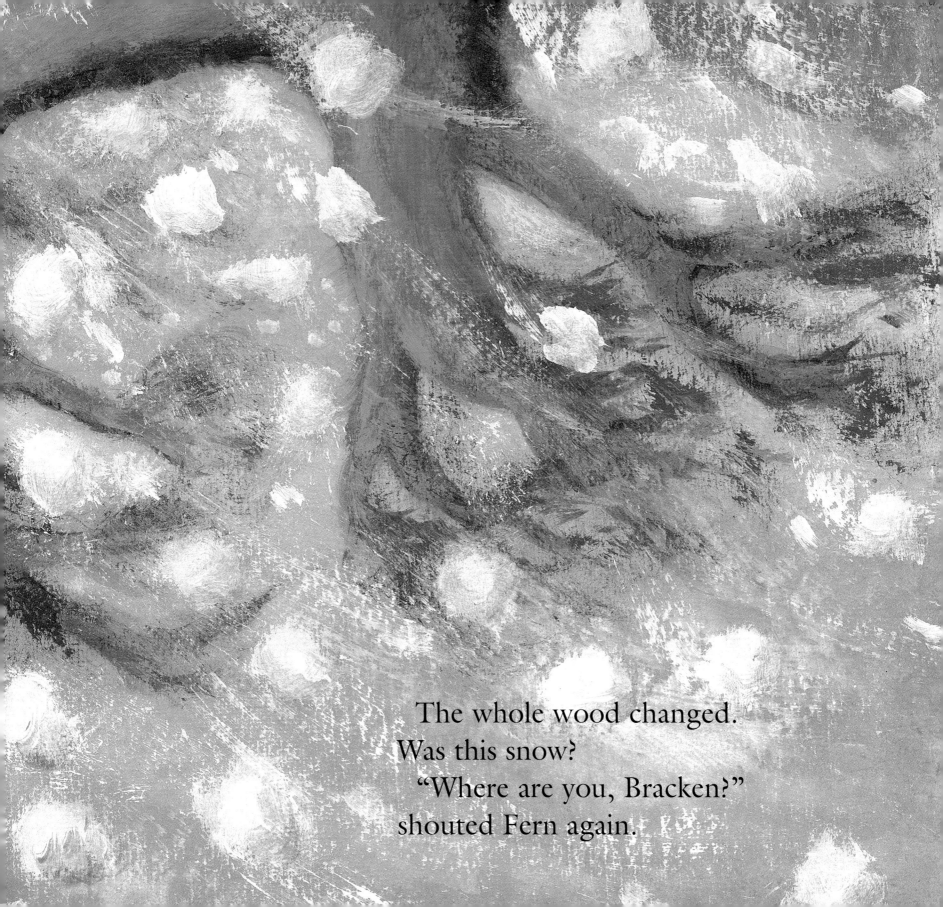

The whole wood changed.
Was this snow?
"Where are you, Bracken?"
shouted Fern again.

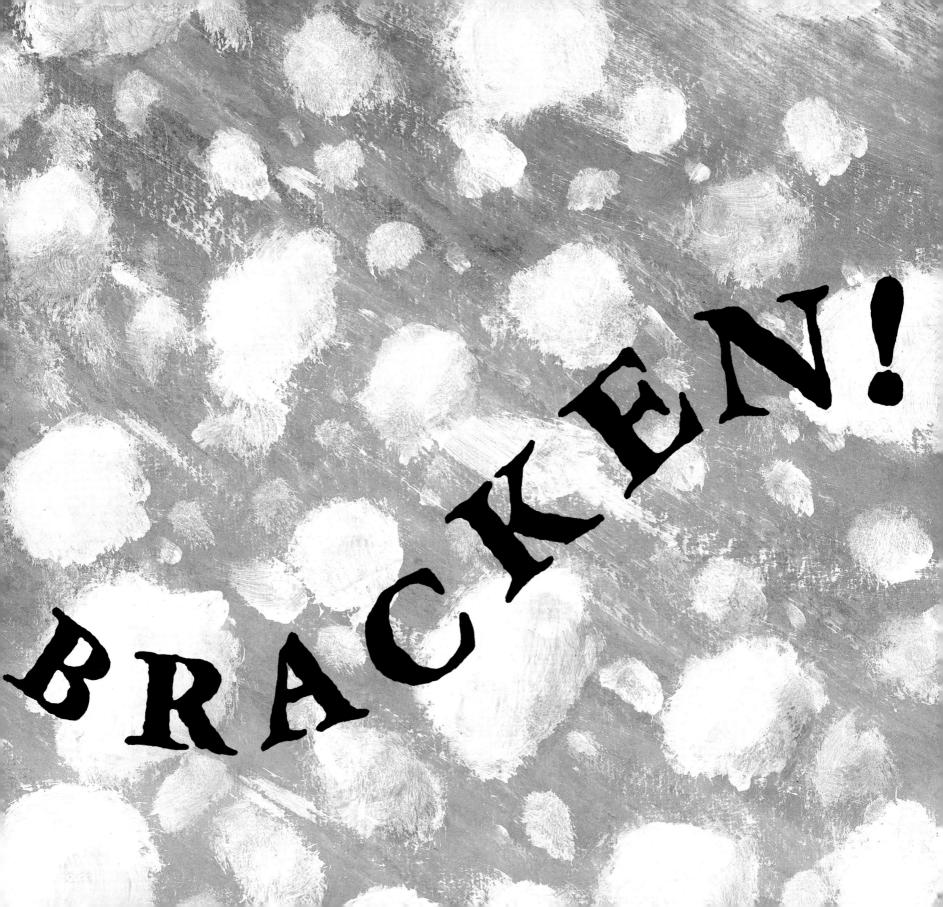

BRACKEN!

"Fern," came a faint cry deep
in the snow. It was Bracken!
Fern dug and dug and dug . . .

and there at last was Bracken.

"What's happening?" he said, trembling.

"I think the snow has come," said Fern. "Ma says it's lovely when it settles."

And they huddled up as close as close could be until it stopped snowing.

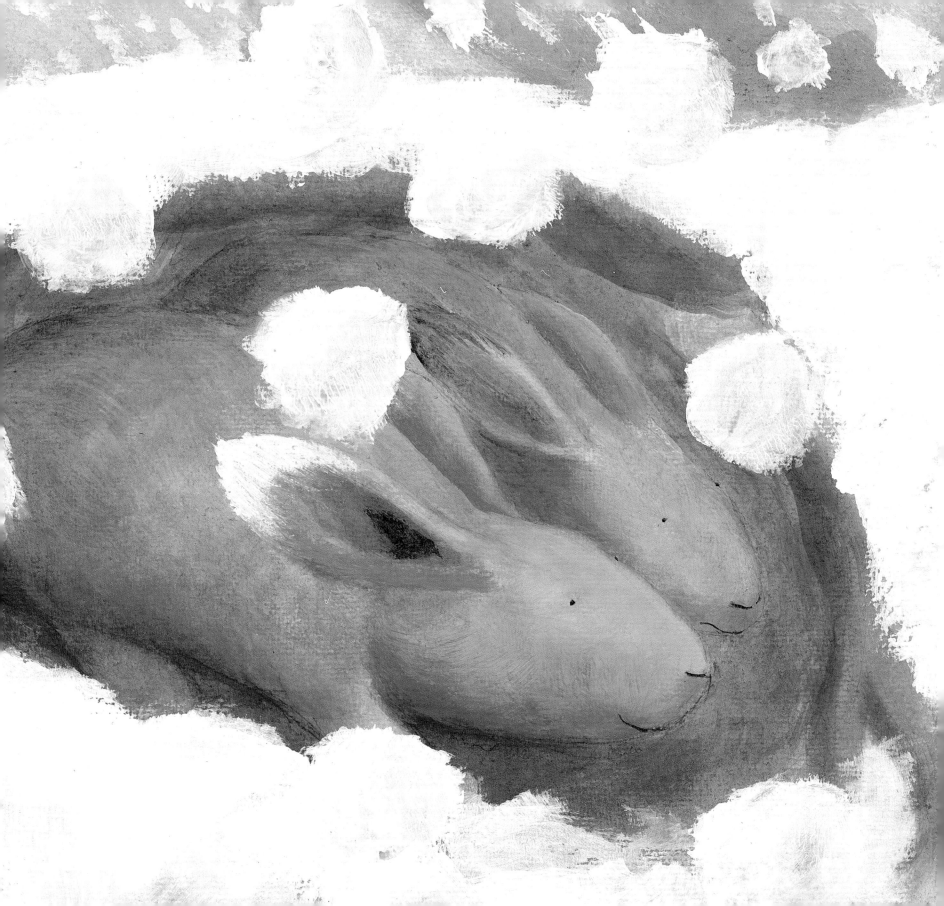

Then they hopped and flipped
and giggled in the fluffy cold snow.
"Fern! Bracken!" called Ma Rabbit.
"Time to come in."

And that night they all curled up as close as close could be in the warm soft hay.